DISCARD

Lee Whedon Memorial Library
020 West Avenue
Medina, NY 14103

What Happens When
Flowers Grow?

What Happens When
Flowers Grow?

Daphne Butler

RAINTREE
STECK-VAUGHN
PUBLISHERS
The Steck-Vaughn Company

Austin, Texas

Lee - Whedon Memorial Library
620 West Avenue
Medina, NY 14103

© Copyright 1996, text, Steck-Vaughn Company

All rights reserved. No part of this book may be reproduced or utilized in any form or by any means, electronic or mechanical, including photocopying, recording, or by any information storage and retrieval system, without permission in writing from the Publisher. Inquiries should be addressed to: Copyright Permissions, Steck-Vaughn Company, P.O. Box 26015, Austin, TX 78755

Published by Raintree Steck-Vaughn Publishers, an imprint of Steck-Vaughn Company

Library of Congress Cataloging-in-Publication Data

Butler, Daphne, 1945–
    What happens when flowers grow? / Daphne Butler.
       p.   cm. — (What happens when—?)
    Includes index.
    ISBN 0-8172-4150-7
    1. Flowers—Juvenile literature. 2. Growth (Plants)—Juvenile literature. 3. Plants—Development—Juvenile literature.
    [1. Flowers. 2. Plants—Development 3. Growth (Plants) 4. Seeds.] I. Title. II. Series: Butler, Daphne, 1945– What happens when—?
    QK49.B95   1996
    582.13'04463—dc20   95-10520
                                                                             CIP
                                                                              AC

Printed and bound in Singapore
1 2 3 4 5 6 7 8 9 0 99 98 97 96 95

Contents

Flowers in the Winter	6
Spring	8
Flowers in the Summer	10
Butterflies and Bees	12
Fruits, Nuts, and Berries	14
Different Seeds	16
What Happens Next?	18
How Do Seeds Grow?	20
How Do Plants Live?	22
Inside a Flower	24
Rare Flowers	26
Flower Words	28
Index	30

Flowers in the Winter

In the winter, the days are fairly short. The sun is low in the sky, and the weather is usually cold and wet. It may even snow.

Trees have no leaves, and most green plants have died away.

Only a few flowers bloom during the winter cold. Do you know any ones that do?

Spring

Trees and plants are brought back to life by gentle rain and the warmth of the sun.

The trees blossom, and flowers push upward from the ground below.

Flowers in the Summer

As spring turns into summer, trees and plants grow rapidly. Flowers bloom in gardens and on hillsides.

Some flowers are grown in fields as crops. Do you know which ones?

Butterflies and Bees

Butterflies and bees fly from flower to flower. They feed on a sweet liquid called **nectar**. They find nectar inside of the flowers.

Bees also collect **pollen**. Pollen is a yellowish dust made by flowers.

Fruits, Nuts, and Berries

When summer turns into fall, flowers die. A fruit is left in their place. Each kind of plant has its own fruit.

Some fruits are soft. Others are hard nuts or tough berries.

Different Seeds

The fruit carries the seeds of the plant. Each kind of plant has its own seed. The fruits of some plants contain many seeds. Other fruits only have one seed.

Do you know the names of these fruits and their seeds?

What Happens Next?

Every plant has a way of spreading its seeds. Some seed pods explode. What other ways can you think of?

When winter comes, the scattered seeds lie in the ground, waiting for the next spring.

The spring sunshine warms the earth. Inside the seed, life stirs.

A root grows into the soil to take in moisture. Soon a green shoot pushes upward, and a new plant is born. This is called **germination**.

How Do Seeds Grow?

How Do Plants Live?

Plants need sunlight and air. They also need water. They get water from the soil through their roots.

The water travels up thin tubes to the leaves. Inside the leaves, water and air join together. Then they make the energy needed for growth.

The green color in the leaves is called **chlorophyll**. It helps to make energy when the sun shines.

Inside a Flower

Flowers have brightly colored petals and a sweet smell. This is why they attract bees and butterflies. As insects move around inside a flower, they scatter its pollen.

Pollen is a yellowish dust made by the **anthers**. When visiting insects spread the pollen to the **stigma,** it is called **pollination**. Seeds can then begin to grow.

Rare Flowers

Plants need the right kinds of places
in which to grow. Some grow in the
woods or by the side of a stream.
If those types of places disappear,
so will the plants.

Without plants, there are no flowers.
Without flowers, there can never be
any seeds to grow new plants.

If the very last plant disappeared,
we would never be able to bring the
flowers back again.

Flower Words

anther The part of the flower that makes the pollen

chlorophyll A colored material that makes plants green

germination The means by which a seed starts to grow

nectar Sweet-smelling juice that attracts bees and butterflies to flowers

shoot
seed
root

pollen Fine yellowish dust found in flowers

pollination The process by which pollen joins with the female part of the flower so that a seed forms

stigma The female part of the flower. It receives the pollen.

bee collecting pollen

pollen sac

bee spreads pollen from anthers to stigma

Index

A
air 23
anther 24, 25, 28, 29

B
bee 12, 25, 29
berries 15
blossom 8
butterflies 12, 25

C
chlorophyll 23, 28
crops 11

E
energy 23

F
fall 15
fruit 15, 17

G
germination 28

I
insects 25

L
leaves 20, 23

N
nectar 12, 28
nuts 15

P
petal 24, 25
plant 7, 15, 17, 19, 20, 23, 27, 28, 29
pollen 12, 24, 25, 29
pollination 29

R
rain 8
root 20, 23, 28

S
seeds 17, 19, 20, 25, 27
soil 20, 23
spring 8, 11, 19, 20

stigma 24, 25, 29
summer 10, 11, 15
sun 7, 8, 20, 23

T
tree 7, 8, 11

W
water 23
winter 7, 19

J582.13 Butl

Butler, Daphne, 1945-

What happens when flowers grow?

LEE-WHEDON MEMORIAL LIBRARY
3 4103 00071 2929

DISCARD

LEE-WHEDON MEMORIAL LIBRARY
MEDINA, NEW YORK

APR 16 1996